TINY TRIUMP
PLEASE WONDERFUL MUMMY

By Anne de Graaf
Illustrated by Evelyn Rivet

Dedicated to Erik

KINGSWAY PUBLICATIONS
EASTBOURNE

Daniel was a naughty boy, but not really.
Julia was a naughty girl, but not really.
  Mummy was tired of calling them naughty, really.

  The two children were naughty because they didn't like saying please and thank you.
  Instead they grunted, or they didn't listen.

  Every day, before work and after, Mummy told them,
  "Say thank you, say please."
  Every time she said it frowns came and chased the smiles away.
  That's when Mummy asked God for more patience.

4

It happened at dinner
when Julia pointed at the potatoes.
"Gimme more."
"Say please," smiled Mummy.
Julia grunted, "Mmf."
Mummy frowned, "Naughty girl."

It happened in the shop when the nice lady gave the children sweets.

"Say thank you to the nice lady."

The children grunted, "Mmf."

Mummy smiled at the nice lady.

But inside Mummy frowned.

It even happened in Grandpa's hospital room, which was no surprise, really, since the frowns had thrown the smiles out of that place a long, long time ago.

When Grandpa gave Julia and Daniel a coin, he frowned.
Mummy tried to smile. "Say thank you."
Julia and Daniel grunted, "Mmf."
Mummy frowned.

On the way home Mummy said,
"You children are very, very naughty. You never say please or thank you. Why should I have such naughty, naughty children?"

Daniel and Julia thought to themselves,
"Maybe we are naughty, but not really."

One day, when Mummy had to go to work and the weather was nice, Mummy's brother Bernard came to visit.

"Here's a present for you, Daniel," Uncle Bernard said.
"Say thank you," whispered Mummy.
"And here's one for you, Julia."
"Say thank you," muttered Mummy.
Nobody listened and Mummy took her frown to work that day.

At dinner that evening Daniel pointed to the potatoes. "Gimme more."

"Say please," smiled Mummy.

Daniel didn't listen.

"What did you say?" Uncle Bernard asked him.

The potatoes steamed at his end of the table.

"Mmf please," said Daniel.

"Please who?" Uncle Bernard's eyes twinkled.

"Please Mummy," said Julia.

"Please what kind of Mummy?"

Mummy looked up. Julia and Daniel shrugged their shoulders.

"What does he mean?"

Uncle Bernard winked at Mummy.

"Please wonderful Mummy."

"Please . . ."

Julia and Daniel giggled. ". . . wonderful Mummy."

A smile ran around the table and chased the frowns away.

This happened in the shop when the nice lady gave the children sweets.

"Say thank you to the nice lady."

"Thank you wonderful, nice lady."

Mummy smiled.

But inside Mummy laughed.

This even happened in Grandpa's hospital room.

When Grandpa gave Julia and Daniel a coin,
he frowned.
"Thank you wonderful Grandpa."
And, for the first time in a long, long while . . .
Grandpa smiled.

That's when the smiles threw the frowns out of
that place for good.

On the way home Mummy cried.
She called them good tears.
"Thank you for making Grandpa smile like that."

"Thank you who?"
grinned the children.
Mummy looked up.
Julia and Daniel winked.

"Thank you wonderful
Julia and Daniel."

Daniel and Julia thought
to themselves,
"Yes, we are wonderful."

Now, every day, before work and after, Mummy tells them,
"Please remember to say thank you, wonderful children."
Every time she says it, smiles come and chase the frowns away.

That's when Mummy thanks God for his patience.

Daniel is a wonderful boy, really.
Julia is a wonderful girl, really.
And wonderful Mummy likes calling them wonderful, really.